Turkeys Together

by Carol Wallace

illustrated by Jacqueline Rogers

SCHOLASTIC INC.

New York Toronto London Auckland Sydney
Mexico City New Delhi Hong Kong Buenos Aires

To Our *little turkeys*
Jordan Paige and William James
C. W.

For Lucas
with a special thanks to Betty Kern
and her Beautiful Pointer, Jack
J. R.

ISBN-13: 978-0-439-89516-3
ISBN-10: 0-439-89516-2

Text copyright © 2005 by Carol Wallace.
Illustrations copyright © 2005 by Jacqueline Rogers. All rights reserved.
Published by Scholastic Inc., 557 Broadway, New York, NY 10012,
by arrangement with Holiday House, Inc.
SCHOLASTIC and associated logos are trademarks
and/or registered trademarks of Scholastic Inc.

12 11 10 9 8 7 6 5 4 3 2 1   6 7 8 9 10 11/0

Printed in the U.S.A.   23

First Scholastic printing, November 2006

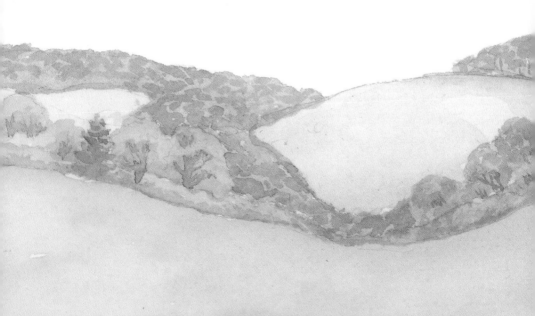

Contents

1. Go Away, Dog

Sniff, sniff, sniff.

I followed the scent.

"Hey, Dog, what are you looking for?"
a small voice called.

"Birds," I answered.

"Why?" the small voice asked.

"I'm a Pointer bird dog," I answered.

"I look for quail.

You are not a quail, are you?"

"I'm a hummingbird," the voice said.

Then the tiny bird flew away.

Sniff, sniff, sniff.

I whiffed the ground.

"Tweet," a whistle came from above me.

"What are you looking for, Dog?"

I looked around.

"*Tweet,*" the whistle came again.

"You are not a quail.

Are you a hummingbird?" I asked.

"I am a big, mean, strong mockingbird,"
the bird said.

"Go look for quail someplace else."

The mockingbird flew away.

Sniff, sniff, sniff.

I followed my nose.

"Gobble!" Feathered wings puffed up.

"You smell like a bird," I said.

"You live on the ground, like a quail.
But you are way too big."

"I'm a turkey. Mother Turkey to you.
Go away!"

She shook her wings.

She meant business.

"I'm a Pointer.

I'm supposed to find birds," I said.

"Listen, Dog.

I have to protect my nest," she said.

"Someone has been taking my eggs.

No dog is going to point at me."

I took a step forward.

"Do you have any babies yet?"
The bird's big wings flapped
in my face.
Her big feet hit my back.
I ran home as fast as I could go.

2. Find That Thief

Sniff, sniff, sniff.

I was close to the nest.

Mother Turkey crouched low

in the tall grass.

"Mother Turkey, it's me.

May I see your eggs?"

I stepped closer.

"Look, Dog.

Someone stole another one of my eggs.

I can't even leave my nest.

I can't find food for myself.

Go away."

"How many eggs do you have?"

I asked.

"There are only seven now.

I had thirteen."

Mother Turkey fluffed her feathers.

"Who do you think took your eggs?"

I asked.

"Maybe a skunk.

I don't know."

She looked very sad.

I jumped to my feet.

"I'll find your eggs!"

"Just stay away from my nest."

Mother Turkey settled down

on the eggs.

I sniffed high.

I sniffed low.

I kept my nose to the ground.

"*Wwwwolf!*" I barked at Raccoon.

"Do you have Mother Turkey's eggs?"

Raccoon hissed.

"I don't have anybody's eggs."

Raccoon waddled off.

Sniff, sniff, sniff.

I smelled something new.

It was *not* a good smell!

Mama Skunk and her four babies

pranced by.

Their noses were in the air.

Their bushy tails were straight up.

But they had not seen

Mother Turkey's eggs.

3. Mrs. Turkey

I headed back home.

I would find those eggs tomorrow.

Suddenly, I smelled something.

Sniff, sniff, sniff.

I wiggled my nose.

"Hey, Mother Turkey.

Where are you going?"

I called to her.

The big turkey turned around.

"I'm Mrs. Turkey.

Who are you?"

The turkey fluffed her feathers.

"I . . . I'm Dog.

I'm looking for your missing eggs.

Did you forget?" I asked.

"How did you know about my eggs?"

the turkey wanted to know.

"You told me this morning.

Don't you remember?" I asked.

"Opossum took my eggs.

He's already taken five of them.

I had ten. But . . . I didn't tell you."

I looked at her carefully.

"You're not my Mother Turkey."

"I am *Mrs.* Turkey. I have to go."

I watched as the big turkey hustled
through the brush.

Then I ran as fast as I could
to Mother Turkey's nest.

4. The Best Nest in the World

"Mother Turkey. It's me.
I know what happened to your eggs!"
I barked.
"Oh no. Not you again."
Mother Turkey covered
her eggs carefully.

"I found another turkey.

Someone is stealing her eggs, too.

I have an idea."

"I don't want to lose another egg,"

she said. "What is your idea?"

"The other turkey says that

Opossum is stealing her eggs.

She's afraid to leave her nest, too."

Mother Turkey looked up at me.

"So, what should we do?"

"Let's put the nests together.
That way one can sit on all the eggs.
The other can watch and
hunt for food."

"I don't know," Mother Turkey said.

"My babies won't know
their real mother."

"If you don't, you might not
have any babies.
I can help you," I said.
I ran back and forth between
the two nests.

Then the turkeys talked it over.

They liked each other.

Once they decided to let me help,

things went pretty fast.

"Be careful with my eggs.
  Don't bite down,"
  Mrs. Turkey directed.
"I'll be very careful.
  I know how to retrieve."
  Gently, I took an egg in my mouth.
  Mrs. Turkey stood guard
  at her nest.
  I moved each egg
  to Mother Turkey's nest.
"Put it right here, Dog."
  Mother Turkey leaned over
  to give me room.
  I set down the egg
  under her soft feathers.
"Can't let them get too cool,"
  she said.

I picked up the last egg.

Mrs. Turkey followed me

to Mother Turkey's nest.

"Hello, dear," said Mother Turkey.

"Please sit on the nest.

I will go for a short hunt.

I think we have the best eggs

in the world. Don't you?"

Mother Turkey stood over the nest.
She gently climbed over the eggs
and sat down.
"I believe it is the best nest
in the whole world."

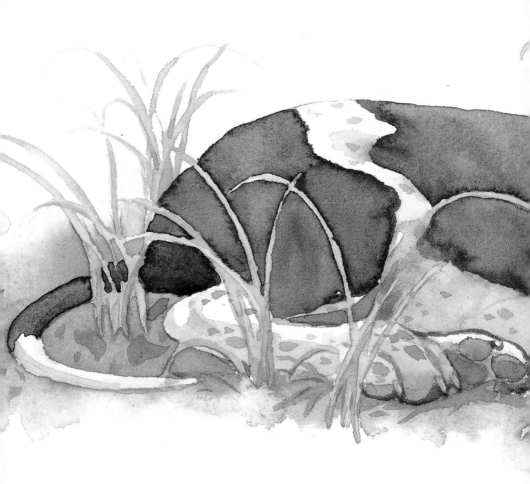

Sometimes, when I was not looking
for quail, I would come and
watch the nest.
Then Mrs. Turkey
and Mother Turkey could get
something to eat.

The eggs finally hatched.
Mother Turkey was right.
The babies weren't sure who
their mother was.

Sometimes they followed Mrs. Turkey.

Sometimes they followed
Mother Turkey.

Sometimes they followed me.

That was fine.

We all loved our babies very much.